PEOPLE OF
THE PLATEAU

by
LINDA THOMPSON

Rourke
Publishing LLC
Vero Beach, Florida 32964

www.rourkepublishing.com

PHOTO CREDITS:
Edward S. Curtis Collection: cover, title page, pages 6-8, 10, 12, 15-17, 21, 23-26, 30-34, 36-38, 40, 42, 43; Courtesy Andreas Trawny: page 4; ; Courtesy of The Division of Anthropology, American Museum of Natural History (AMNH): pages 7, 13, 15, 23, 25, 31, 38, 40, 41 Courtesy U.S. Fish & Wildlife Service: pages 8, 24; Courtesy of Eastern Washington State Historical Society: pages 9, 11, 27; Courtesy of the University of Washington Libraries: pages 13, 16; Courtesy of USGS by Lyn Topinka: page 18; Courtesy Charles Reasoner: pages 19, 22, 34, 35; National Anthropological Archives, Smithsonian Institution: 7, 28, 32, 39, 43.

DESIGN AND LAYOUT by Rohm Padilla, Mi Casa Publications, printing@taosnet.com

Library of Congress Cataloging-In-Publication Data

Thompson, Linda, 1941-
  People of the Plateau / by Linda Thompson.
     v. cm. -- (Native peoples, native lands)
Includes bibliographical references and index.
Contents: The Plateau People today -- Where they came from -- Life on the Plateau -- What they believe.
  ISBN 1-58952-758-5 (hardcover)
  1. Indians of North America--Great Basin--History--Juvenile literature. 2. Indians of North America--Great Basin--Social life and customs--Juvenile literature. [1. Indians of North America--Great Basin.] I. Title. II. Series: Thompson, Linda, 1941-   Native peoples, Native lands.
  E78.G67T46 2003
  979.5004'97--dc22
                                        2003011782

Printed in the U.S.A.

TITLE PAGE IMAGE
Old Time Warrior, a Nez Perce man photographed by Edward Curtis

TABLE OF CONTENTS

Coquihalla Highway,
British Columbia,
Canada

Chapter I:
THE PLATEAU PEOPLE

*T*he **Plateau People** live in Washington, Oregon, Idaho, western Montana, and British Columbia, Canada. They descended from more than two dozen Native American tribes who lived on the Columbia Plateau before Christopher Columbus "discovered" America in 1492. Because Columbus landed on the eastern edge of the American continent, several centuries would pass before the Plateau People were also "discovered" by Europeans.

Perhaps 200,000 Plateau People once occupied this region, but today only about 45,000 of their descendants remain. The country consists of **tablelands** and mountains with scanty forests and a network of streams and lakes created by two great rivers, the Columbia and the Snake. A century or more ago, people wandered freely, hunting and fishing as they liked, trading with other tribes, and moving their camps as the seasons changed. Today, like other Native people across North America, the Plateau People mostly live on **reservations.**

Snake River, on the
Idaho–Oregon border
photo by Andreas Trawny

4

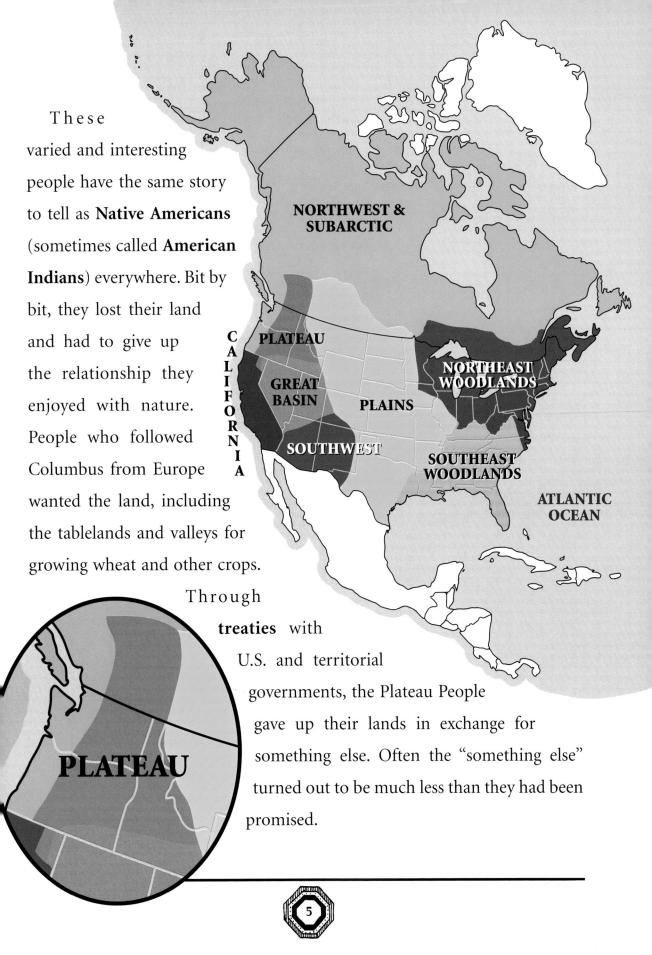

These varied and interesting people have the same story to tell as **Native Americans** (sometimes called **American Indians**) everywhere. Bit by bit, they lost their land and had to give up the relationship they enjoyed with nature. People who followed Columbus from Europe wanted the land, including the tablelands and valleys for growing wheat and other crops. Through **treaties** with U.S. and territorial governments, the Plateau People gave up their lands in exchange for something else. Often the "something else" turned out to be much less than they had been promised.

NORTHWEST & SUBARCTIC

PLATEAU

C A L I F O R N I A

GREAT BASIN

PLAINS

NORTHEAST WOODLANDS

SOUTHWEST

SOUTHEAST WOODLANDS

ATLANTIC OCEAN

PLATEAU

As Europeans and their descendants pressed west, they urged their government to open up more land for settlement. The U.S. Government persuaded Plateau leaders to sign treaties that created reservations. Some leaders disagreed with the terms of these treaties, and only a few would sign them. Still, the government made the treaties apply to everyone. The Native peoples were usually given two choices: to move to a reservation or be destroyed by war.

Reservations were usually created on the least desirable land, where game and water were scarce. Dishonest suppliers often cheated Natives out of their provisions. Also, Europeans tried to force the Native people to become farmers, an idea very strange to them because for centuries they had followed a **nomadic** way of life.

**On the
Spokane River in 1910**

Nez Perce war club made of wood, hide, fur, feathers, and stone

Naturally, individuals had different opinions about how to resist the takeover of their territory. Some wanted to live peaceably with the settlers and had friends among them. But others distrusted the newcomers and wanted to fight for their lands and their way of life. These disagreements led wise chieftains, like Chief Joseph of the Nez Perce [Nez Pierce] tribe and "Captain Jack" of the Modoc, into wars.

Ahlakat, a Nez Perce man and nephew of Chief Joseph, in 1907. He was born in 1860.

Chief Joseph

Chief Joseph of the Nez Perce believed everyone could live in harmony. But as Natives were forced from their land, he changed his mind. When war broke out in 1877, the Nez Perce tried to escape to Canada. But the Army trapped them in Montana. After several bloody battles, Joseph surrendered. His speech, now famous, ends: "Hear me, my chiefs! I am tired; my heart is sick and sad. From where the sun now stands I will fight no more forever."

Wishham man with a catch of salmon

King salmon

The Treaty of 1855 gave Plateau tribes fishing rights in exchange for land. But new laws violated treaty rights and hydroelectric plants and dams interfered with salmon migration. Court decisions wore away Native fishing rights. Finally, in 1994, the Nez Perce, Umatilla, Warm Springs, and Yakima tribes developed a fish restoration program that includes hatcheries and watershed protection. It is called Wy-Kan-Ush-Mi Wa-Kish-Wit: Spirit of the Salmon.

It was very difficult for the Plateau People to adjust to reservation life. Tribes that considered salmon an important food lost many fishing grounds in the early 1900s when the government built dams on the Columbia. Hunting restrictions brought additional hardship. No longer able to depend on hunting and fishing, Native people had to take jobs outside of their communities. This new way of life broke up the close-knit families and groups that had been used to working together.

Nez Perce children at a boarding school in Lawpai, Idaho, around 1900

These days, Plateau People live in houses, drive cars, watch television, and eat many of the same foods that other Americans eat. Children go to public schools and their parents work at a variety of jobs. But to maintain the family cooperation and closeness they once had, families still come together for **powwows** and rodeos, and they try to take time off from jobs and schools to attend these gatherings.

Members of different Plateau tribes prepare for a War Dance at a powwow around 1900.

Although the sizes and shapes of reservations have changed over the years, one thing is generally true. Each U.S. reservation has its own government with a **sovereign nation** status. This means that people living there have their own laws and tribal organizations, and in many ways are not subject to U.S. or state laws. For example, reservations have created gambling **casinos** in states where gambling is otherwise illegal. The casinos create jobs and provide money for schools and other programs to raise the standard of living.

Thousands of Plateau descendants have merged into the general population, but many still live on reservations. In British Columbia, Canada, Native village sites became small **reserves** for tribes such as the Thompson, the Shuswap, and the Lillooet.

Many modern Native villages and reservations are close to settlers' cities and towns. In this 1911 photo, a Kalispel village sits opposite the town of Cusick, Washington.

The larger Plateau reservations in Washington are the Colville, the Spokane, and the Yakima. In Oregon, the Warm Springs and Umatilla reservations are home to several thousand people. The Nez Perce and Coeur d'Alene tribes have large reservations in Idaho. Some peoples who once lived in eastern Washington, Idaho, and Montana are combined on the Flathead Reservation in western Montana.

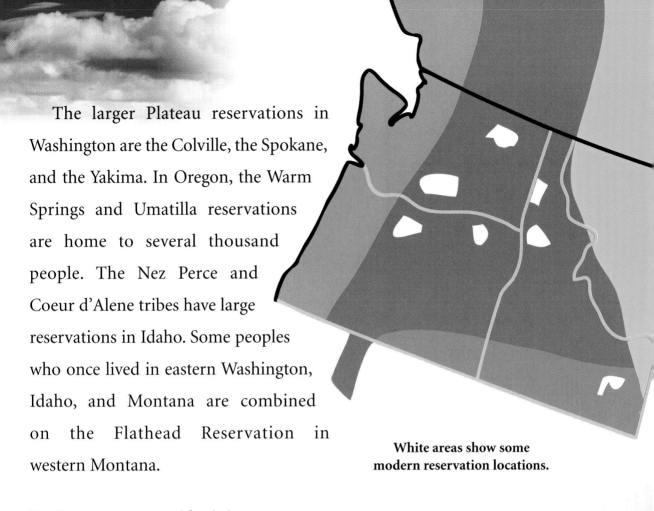

White areas show some modern reservation locations.

Nez Perce encampment with mission church, tipis, and town buildings visible

Wherever they live, Native peoples are actively engaged in preserving their heritage. For example, they still make traditional clothing, bags, baskets, **drums,** and other items used for ceremonies. Some tribes continue to practice their spiritual customs. And young people are learning tribal languages, songs, **dances,** and ceremonies. They understand that by engaging in these things, they can keep their history and values alive.

Today, non-native people can attend feasts and powwows and learn about Plateau People. The Confederated Tribes of the Umatilla hold powwows and rodeos near Pendleton, Oregon. In Washington, both the Confederated Tribes of the Colville and the Spokane people sponsor dances, games, and powwows. At the Flathead Reservation's annual powwow in Montana, Natives sing in groups, accompanied by **drumming,** to the Owl, Grass, Tea, and Rabbit dances.

Flathead war dance

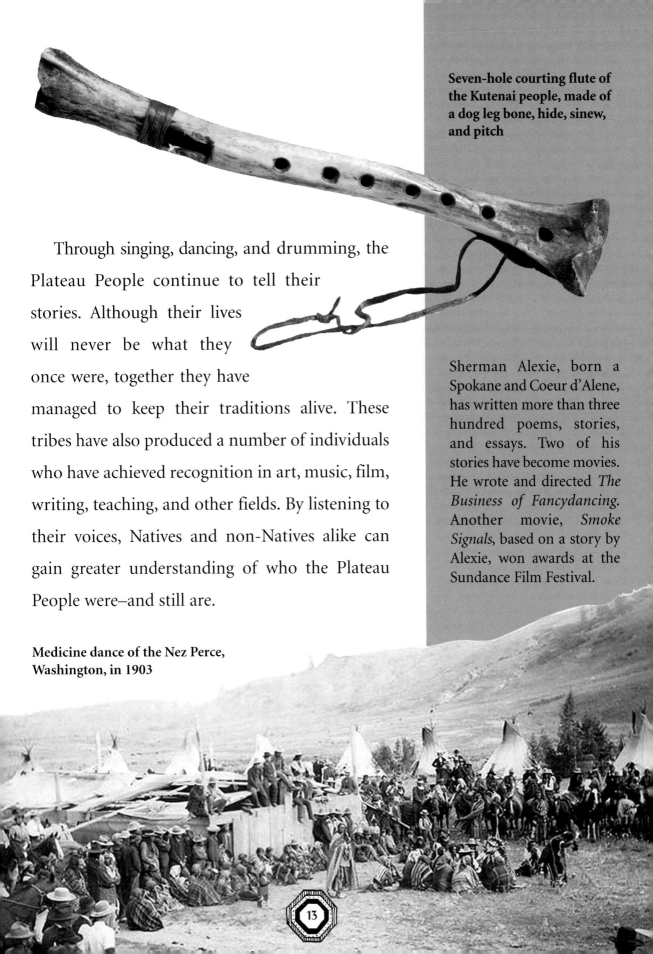

Seven-hole courting flute of the Kutenai people, made of a dog leg bone, hide, sinew, and pitch

Through singing, dancing, and drumming, the Plateau People continue to tell their stories. Although their lives will never be what they once were, together they have managed to keep their traditions alive. These tribes have also produced a number of individuals who have achieved recognition in art, music, film, writing, teaching, and other fields. By listening to their voices, Natives and non-Natives alike can gain greater understanding of who the Plateau People were–and still are.

Sherman Alexie, born a Spokane and Coeur d'Alene, has written more than three hundred poems, stories, and essays. Two of his stories have become movies. He wrote and directed *The Business of Fancydancing*. Another movie, *Smoke Signals*, based on a story by Alexie, won awards at the Sundance Film Festival.

Medicine dance of the Nez Perce, Washington, in 1903

◄BERING STRAIT

Chapter II:

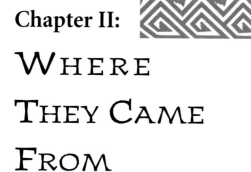

WHERE THEY CAME FROM

Scientists believe that Native Americans descended from Asian people who walked across land or ice bridges beginning perhaps 30,000 years ago. It is also possible that some came by boat. A land **migration** would have occurred at the Bering Strait, a narrow waterway between Siberia (a part of Russia) and the present state of Alaska. Sea levels might have been lower then, exposing land.

Early native people would have used chipped stone arrowheads and tools.

Buckskin dress

This rock was used as a slide by children.

Within a few thousand years, descendants of these **immigrants** had spread across North, Central, and South America. They divided into hundreds of different groups, speaking many languages. In some areas, they hunted huge **mammoths** and other great animals that are now extinct. Some groups lived as nomads, wandering great distances in search of food. If water was plentiful and they could grow food, they settled down.

Native people adapted well to their environment. They used natural materials around them to make tools and clothing, to feed themselves, and to build shelters. Early Plateau People built houses from brush, reeds, and wood. Later, when the horse was introduced, they could travel further and hunt large animals such as elk and bison. Then they began to make **tipis** and clothing out of skins. Some tribes made hats and baskets out of corn husks, grass, reeds, or other plant fibers. Women wore **buckskin** dresses decorated with seeds and shells.

Chinook man standing on the bank of the Columbia River at the landing place of Lewis and Clark

From as early as 1750, the Plateau People began to see a few explorers from Spain, France, and England travel through their lands. In 1805 and 1806, Meriwether Lewis and William Clark led an expedition down the Columbia River. Its purpose was to map new lands, to seek a waterway to the Pacific, and to study the Indians. In their journals, Lewis and Clark wrote that they met friendly members of the Nez Perce and Walla Walla tribes. Most Native peoples welcomed and helped these explorers, giving them food and horses and acting as scouts along the way.

Nez Perce hunting party meets a government surveyor. Engraving made in 1853 by J. M. Stanley

What Do the Plateau People Believe about How They Came to America?

Tsagiglalal, the guardian of Nihhluidih

The Plateau People have their own stories about how they originated. Most North American tribes believed that the first parents came either from underground or from the sky. In the case of the Plateau tribes, the Creator is often called the "Great Chief Above" or the "Chief Sky Spirit."

The Modoc tell how the Chief Sky Spirit carved a hole in the sky and pushed snow and ice through it, creating Mount Shasta in California. He and his family went down to live inside the mountain. Whatever he touched with his walking stick became alive. He made birds, fish, beaver, bears, trees, and rivers. He built a fire inside Mount Shasta and made a hole in the top so the smoke and sparks from his fire could fly out. This description reminds us that Mount Shasta, an extinct volcano, once erupted with fire and smoke bursting out of its peak.

Natives had many spiritual stories to explain the natural activities occurring around them.

Mount Shasta, California
USGS photo by Lyn Topinka

Old Man of the Ancients and his daughter

Another Modoc story says that Kumush, Old Man of the Ancients, took his daughter to the underground world of the spirits. He brought up bones, which on Earth turned into all of the different Plateau Peoples. When he spoke or thought the names of all the birds, fish, plants, and animals, each one appeared. Then, from the eastern edge of the world, he followed the sun's path to the middle of the sky. There he built a house for his daughter and himself.

An important figure in the beliefs of the people of this region is "Coyote." A story from the Colville people tells how Coyote made the Columbia River.

Long ago, when Coyote was the Big Man on the earth, this valley was covered by a big lake. There was no Columbia River. Instead, between the lake and the ocean was a long ridge of mountains. Coyote was smart enough to see that salmon would come up from the ocean if he would make a hole through those mountains. So he went down to a place near where Portland, Oregon, is now, and with his powers he dug a hole through the mountains. The lake flowed out through the hole into the ocean, and became the Columbia River. After the salmon swam up the river, the people had plenty to eat.

The creation stories told by a tribe or a nation attempt to explain how people and everything else on Earth came into existence. These are just a few among the countless tales that the Plateau People pass from generation to generation to make sure that their history, ancient knowledge, and culture survive.

Coyote on the prowl

Chapter III

LIFE ON THE PLATEAU

House made of reed mats and wood poles

*B*efore they had horses, most Plateau People lived in cone-shaped houses or rectangular lodges called **longhouses**. The longhouse is like an A-frame house up to 90 feet (27 m) long, with **gables** formed by long poles at two ends. Both types of houses had roofs made of brush or woven **tule** reeds or cattails. When a family moved, they took the mats and left the poles behind. It was easy to put up a new set of poles at the next camp.

A feast was held in an extended tipi to honor Chief Joseph after his death in 1904.

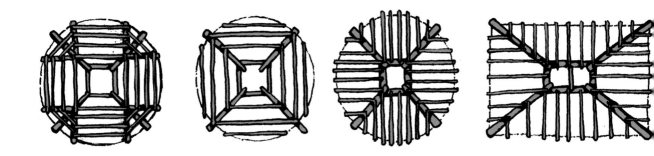

Some of the common variations of roof framing for Thompson pit houses

After the horse came to the Plateau, some tribes, such as the Flathead, began to live in tipis made of animal skins, carrying the skins on horses when they moved. But in winter, they returned to their permanent lodges, which were warm and large enough for their food and belongings.

The most northern tribes in this region, such as the Thompson, Okanagan, and Lillooet, lived in mounded, partly buried houses called the **Thompson pit house**. People entered the house by climbing down a roof ladder.

Cross section of a Thompson
pit house

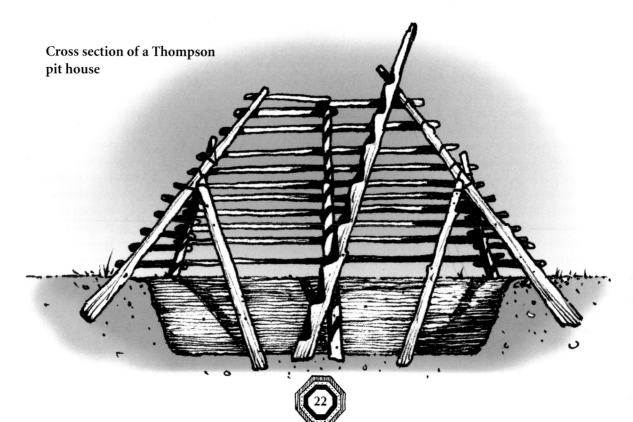

Dipnets like this could also be attached to long wooden poles for fishing.

In the spring, **bands** of Natives living near the Columbia River and other rivers gathered to fish for salmon. They dried some of the salmon for later use and for trading. Salmon made up a third of Plateau Peoples' diet, and they even boiled the skins to make glue. In some areas, Plateau People stood on wooden platforms hung from rocks above the river to catch salmon with long-handled **dipnets**. In other parts of the Plateau, nets, spears, or traps were used. The women's job was to clean the fish and hang them on racks to dry in the sun.

Wishham man with a long-handled dipnet on a wooden fishing platform

In spring, these groups moved to higher elevations to dig for roots, which they also dried. An important root was the **camas**, an edible lily bulb. Some types were used in ways similar to onions, and other types were ground for flour. In the late summer, the bands moved even higher into the mountains to pick berries and hunt for deer and elk. More than 22 types of berries were eaten, including chokecherries and huckleberries.

As autumn approached, people returned to the Columbia River and its tributaries for the salmon run. Salmon are born in fresh water and swim to the ocean, where they live until they are ready to **spawn**. In the fall, they return upstream to where they were born. Like today's anglers, Native fishermen were eager to catch these large salmon as they swam home.

Fishing for salmon with a spear

Lakeshore tribes such as the Coeur d'Alene (Schitsu'umsh in their own language) fished for lake species such as mountain whitefish, sockeye salmon, and steelhead trout. They used canoes made out of long strips of pine or cedar bark to fish and travel among their lakeside winter camps.

Canoe pulled ashore on the banks of Flathead Lake, Montana

Steelhead trout

Plateau Peoples decorated their clothing and other objects with beautiful designs. They wove strong bags for gathering food and adorned them with beads and porcupine quills. They made **moccasins** from animal skins and arrows from wood and stone. While they generally did not plant crops, they used deer and elk antlers to dig wild roots. They were very skilled at weaving reeds and fibers into baskets, which they used in many ways. The women even wove baskets into packs for carrying babies safely on their backs. Food was cooked in baskets by first pouring water in, then dropping hot rocks into the basket until the water boiled.

Beaded leather moccasins

Lillooet woven basket

Nez Perce baby on cradle-board

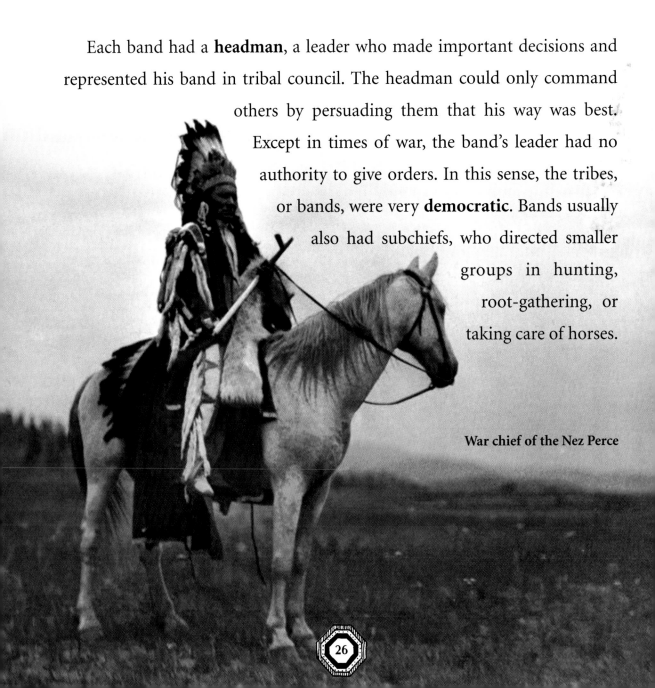

Parents, children, aunts, uncles, cousins, and grandparents lived together in a band. Everyone had a job to do, and if someone failed to do a good job, the band might freeze or go hungry during the winter. The men and boys hunted and fished and made arrows, weapons, and tools. They also took care of the horses. The women and girls set up tipis, cooked, dried fish and meat, dug roots, picked berries, and made clothes and decorations.

Each band had a **headman**, a leader who made important decisions and represented his band in tribal council. The headman could only command others by persuading them that his way was best. Except in times of war, the band's leader had no authority to give orders. In this sense, the tribes, or bands, were very **democratic**. Bands usually also had subchiefs, who directed smaller groups in hunting, root-gathering, or taking care of horses.

War chief of the Nez Perce

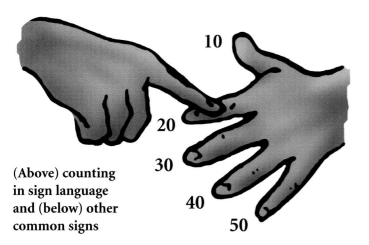

(Above) counting in sign language and (below) other common signs

One European influence on Plateau People came from a powerful English business, the Hudson's Bay Company. It had been operating east of the Rockies since 1670 and was mostly interested in furs. The company began trading with Plateau tribes in about 1821, when it merged with its biggest competitor, the North West Company. Today, the Hudson's Bay Company has large department stores all over Canada.

Although the many tribes of the Plateau spoke different languages, they traveled widely, trading and visiting. They also intermarried, adopting elements from each other's cultures. If they spoke different languages, people communicated through **sign language**. Trading was important because this region lay at the center of a vast network where Plains, Northwest Coast, and California peoples came to exchange goods.

Blockhouse at the old fort of the Hudson's Bay Trading Co., near Colville, Washington. Established in 1854 for protection from Natives.

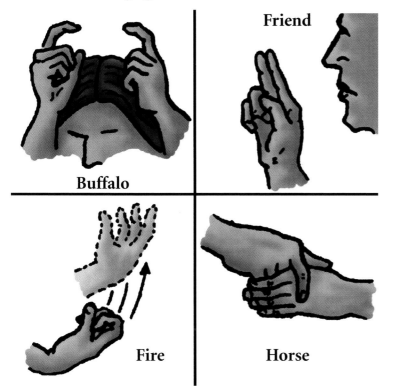

Buffalo

Friend

Fire

Horse

In the 1740s, Plateau People began to use horses and became more nomadic. Some tribes such as the Cayuse and Nez Perce became adept at horse breeding. The Nez Perce bred the first **Appaloosa** horses.

Europeans who brought the horse to America also introduced three other things that had an immense influence on Native peoples—the rifle, Christianity, and contagious diseases. When Natives used rifles instead of spears or bows and arrows to settle quarrels, the results were much more serious. Catholic and Protestant **missionaries** brought Christianity to Native peoples, teaching them that their ancient ways of living and believing were wrong. Chapter IV tells more about the Plateau Peoples' beliefs and how their lives and beliefs are intertwined.

The worst thing Europeans brought was disease. Native people had no immunity to new diseases such as smallpox and measles, and thousands became ill and died. On the Plateau, the effects were most tragic along the Columbia River, a major trade route. When Europeans first came to trade, their diseases nearly wiped some tribes out of existence.

Group of Nez Perce on horseback in 1906

Spanish mission church

In 1847, a group of Cayuse murdered missionaries Marcus and Narcissa Whitman, burning their mission. The Cayuse blamed the Whitmans for a measles epidemic that had killed hundreds of Cayuse and others. Before the leaders were hanged, one said, "Did not your missionaries teach us that Christ died to save his people? So die we to save our people."

Some Plateau Tribes

One large tribe, the Nez Perce, who called themselves the Ni míi puu [Nee-Me-Poo], lived near the Bitterroot Mountains in Idaho and in northeastern Oregon. Nez Perce is French for "pierced nose." Although the Ni míi puu did not pierce their noses, some Europeans mistook them for a tribe that did practice nose-piercing. There were about 6,000 Nez Perce in the early 1800s, but their population fell because of wars and disease. In 2002, 3,296 members were counted.

Nez Perce man maneuvering a dugout canoe with a long wooden pole

Kutenai man hunting from a canoe on Flathead Lake, Montana

The Flathead lived in western Montana. They called themselves the Salish. They also received their European name because of their appearance. Unlike some tribes, they didn't deform their babies' foreheads by pressing them while in the cradle with cone-shaped wooden "hats." Because their heads were not forced into a pointed shape, Europeans called them "flatheads."

The Flathead traded in furs and generally were friendly to Europeans. In the 1840s, Roman Catholic and Protestant missionaries worked hard to convert the Flathead to Christianity. Sent to a reservation near Flathead Lake, Montana, they eventually merged with the Spokane, Kalispel, and other tribes to form the "Confederated Salish-Kutenai" of the Flathead Reservation. In 2002, there were about 6,800 tribal members living on or near the reservation.

Flathead buckskin shirt

Canoes on the Columbia River

"Captain Jack"

When sent to the Klamath Reservation, the Modoc clashed with the Klamath tribe. In 1870, the leader of the Modoc, Kintpuash, or "Captain Jack," led part of his tribe back to their old homelands. They hid out for several months, but a Modoc subchief betrayed them. Captain Jack surrendered and was hanged, with three others.

Toby Riddle Winema arranged a peace council between her cousin Captain Jack and a government agent.

The Colville lived on the Columbia River just south of what is now the Canadian border. In 1872, they were moved to the Colville Reservation in Washington. Many other tribes joined them there, becoming the "Confederated Tribes of the Colville Reservation." In 2002, their population was 8,507, with about half living on the reservation.

The Modoc lived around Lower Klamath Lake, Tule Lake, and Clear Lake in Oregon and northern California. In the early 1870s, they fought hard to stay in their homeland. They were sent to Indian Territory, but eventually the 51 survivors were allowed to return. A few hundred Modoc descendants now live on or near the former Klamath Reservation in Oregon. Including the Klamath and Yahooskin, about 3,000 Natives live there.

The Cayuse, Umatilla, and Walla Walla make up the Confederated Tribes of the Umatilla Indian Reservation near Pendleton, Oregon. Before 1855, more than 8,000 people shared 6.4 million acres (2.59 million ha) in southeastern Washington and northeastern Oregon. Now, a few thousand members live on 172,000 acres (69,600 ha) of their original land.

Cayuse woman in traditional dress

Children were taught traditional ways of life from an early age.

Chapter IV:
WHAT THEY BELIEVE

*A*ll Native peoples' calendars, religion, and legends
are based on nature. Their lives once depended
entirely upon the earth and all that grew on it. To them,
everything on Earth has a spiritual purpose and everything
is interconnected. Although they may have adapted to new ways
and new religions, the old faith remains alive. Their belief that nature
is sacred is evident in their teachings, writings, art, and culture. It is passed
from generation to generation through stories and **ceremonies**.

A ceremonial Crazy Dancer kisses an elder.

A medicine wheel represents the circle of life and many other natural events, such as compass directions, seasons, and elements.

Another central belief among Native peoples has to do with the "sacred hoop" or circle. "The Power of the World always works in circles," said Black Elk, a Native spiritual advisor from another part of the country.

He referred not only to physical circles but also to the cycles of life. When seasons change and the stars, planets, sun, and moon seem to move in repeated patterns, it is part of the never-ending circle. The familiar movements involved in hunting, fishing, and harvesting plants is also a circle. And each generation growing from infancy to youth to adulthood to old age is another. This ever-present circle is also called the **Medicine Wheel**.

Three Eagles of the Nez Perce

On pictures of this wheel, four directions are often represented–north, south, east, and west. These four directions were important in ways of living and believing. South, which has the qualities of warmth and growth, is the season of the infant. West, characterized by rain, is the place for looking within oneself. It is the season of the young person and of the **vision quest** to connect with the Great Spirit. North is the direction of the wind, which represents strength and endurance. In the human cycle, north signifies the wisdom of the adult. Finally, East, symbolizing peace and light, is the season of old age. It is a quiet, reflective period when **elders** can pass along knowledge and experience to young people.

Crater Lake, Oregon

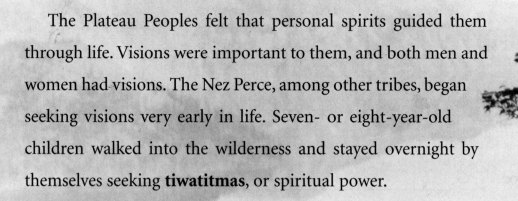

The Plateau Peoples felt that personal spirits guided them through life. Visions were important to them, and both men and women had visions. The Nez Perce, among other tribes, began seeking visions very early in life. Seven- or eight-year-old children walked into the wilderness and stayed overnight by themselves seeking **tiwatitmas**, or spiritual power.

If a young adult tried many times and had received no visions, he or she might resort to purification rituals such as bathing in hot or icy water or tearing their skin with thorns. The Nez Perce believed that these practices made young people better at hunting, healing, and everything else they attempted. However, vision quests were most important for boys training to be warriors, for without a guardian spirit, they would not survive many battles.

Klamath chief praying to the spirits at Crater Lake

Nez Perce bone necklace with stone beads

The Coeur d'Alene call this spiritual power **suumesh**. The early people believed that the Animal Peoples, such as Elk, Wolf or Hawk, might appear and teach a song to the person seeking a vision. This song would guide the person through life. The animal in the vision would become a part of that person's name.

A person with a lot of spiritual power might become a **shaman**, or healer. Shamans lead hunting rituals and ceremonies and preside over burials, among other duties. Both men and women can be shamans.

Cayuse matron wearing a hat made of plant fiber yarn and colored with pigment

Logging train in Spalding Junction, Idaho, in 1903

Early Native peoples could not understand the European view that the earth is something that can be bought and sold. When European-Americans slaughtered the bison from trains or horses, just for entertainment, and left them to rot, Natives watched with astonishment. When settlers cut down forests for houses, plowed up the earth to plant crops, and fenced off the land to keep others out, Natives were shocked. These actions struck deeply at their belief that the earth is sacred.

Skeena Mountain,
British Columbia,
Canada

Today, many Native people are committed to healing the damage that civilization has caused to the natural environment. For instance, the Coeur d'Alene, who have always considered the lakes, rivers, animals, and plants as "family," are taking an active role in cleaning up mining pollution along the Coeur d'Alene River. The Klamath are working to restore the forests and fish that once sustained their people.

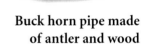

Buck horn pipe made of antler and wood

Religion is acted out through ceremonies. Important ceremonies include smoking of **tobacco** in a **ceremonial pipe** or burning other sacred plants such as **sweetgrass**, **cedar**, or **sage**. Often, the smoke is wafted in the four sacred directions and the last of the tobacco is offered to the Great Spirit.

A Nez Perce sweat lodge

All Native peoples once used tobacco as a sacred ceremonial plant. It might be smoked before a battle or to make peace with former enemies. A pipe ceremony might be held to heal someone, whether present in the group, far away, or deceased. Hunters often smoke a pipe together to show respect for the animals who have died to feed them.

Another ceremony, a type of community prayer, is the **sweat lodge**. Typically, people combine sweating in a heated room with **fasting** and perhaps smoking the sacred pipe. Other ceremonies involve **feasting** on sacred foods. For instance, Plateau People might prepare salmon or camas in a special way.

Tobacco medicine pouch

Sun dance doll of the Kutenai people

When prescribed by an elder, sacred plants can be worn in a **medicine pouch**. The plants are prescribed to call the mercy and protection of the four sacred directions and the Great Spirit to the individual wearing the pouch.

Drums and drumming represent the pulse of the universe. Each drum is considered a sacred object and has a drum-keeper to protect it from casual use. Dances began as ways to tell the story of a hunt or battle. Both men and women still dance traditional dances, including the Fancy Dance and the Grass Dance.

The flight of arrows during a Crazy Dance in 1908

A Klamath drummer with feather headdress

Once, the survival of Native tribes depended on having strong and brave warriors, so warriors' deeds were honored through ceremonies. Today, that feeling is kept alive in the respect shown to veterans of U.S. wars. Native Americans have fought for the United States in every war. Veterans are honored for their willingness to die for their country. Today, powwows and tribal ceremonies often include flag songs and similar observances for Native veterans.

Big Knife of the Flathead. The headdress of buffalo horns and scalp is characteristic of the Plains Indians.

Ahlakat, Ben Beveridge (non-Native), Chief Joseph, and Amos F. Wilkinson

A TIMELINE OF THE HISTORY OF
THE PLATEAU PEOPLE

30,000 to 13,000 BC - Ice ages lower sea levels, making it possible for people to walk across a land bridge from Asia to North America

12,000 to 9,000 BC - Earth warms up and the ice caps melt, allowing people to move throughout North, Central, and South America.

8,000 BC - Early inhabitants are living in the Plateau Region.

AD 1492 - Christopher Columbus arrives in America, near present-day Florida. Thinking he is in India, he names the inhabitants "Indians."

AD 1735 to 1750 - Plateau People acquire horses and become more nomadic. They begin to see occasional European explorers.

AD 1776 - The American Revolution creates a new country, the United States of America.

AD 1803 - United States buys the Louisiana Territory from France for $15 million, doubling the size of the country.

AD 1804 to 1806 - President Thomas Jefferson sends the Lewis and Clark Expedition to explore western lands from St. Louis, Missouri, to the mouth of the Columbia River.

AD 1821 - Hudson's Bay Company merges with the North West Company and the frequency of European trading on the Plateau increases.

AD 1846 - The 49th parallel is selected as the boundary between the United States and Canada.

AD 1847 - The Whitman Massacre.

AD 1855 - The Treaty of 1855 establishes a number of Indian Reservations. It gives some Plateau tribes fishing rights in exchange for land.

AD 1865 - The American Civil War ends with the abolition of slavery.

AD 1869 to 1873 - The Modoc Wars, ending with the hanging of Captain Jack.

AD 1877 - The Nez Perce try to escape to Canada but are forced to surrender in Montana.

AD 1933 to 1942 - The Grand Coulee Dam, the largest of several that interfere with traditional Native fishing, is built on the Columbia River.

AD 1994 - The Nez Perce and other tribes develop a fish restoration program.

GLOSSARY

American Indian - A member of the first peoples of North America.

Appaloosa - A breed of horse developed by the Cayuse.

band - Group of Natives living as a small community; a subdivision of a tribe, sometimes called "tribelet."

buckskin - The skin of a buck (synonym for male deer).

camas A Chinook word for a plant in the lily family with edible roots.

casino - A building used for gambling.

cedar - A member of the pine family of trees, with fragrant, durable wood.

ceremonial pipe - A device for smoking sacred substances, such as tobacco, during a formal event or for an official purpose.

ceremony - A formal act or series of acts.

dance - A series of rhythmic movements, often performed to music.

democratic - Relating to government by the people, especially the rule of the majority.

dipnet - A bag net with a handle, used to scoop fish from the water.

drum - A hollow instrument with coverings, such as skins, over the ends, which can be beaten to make a rhythmic sound. To produce sounds on such an instrument.

drumming - Making a series of strokes or vibrations that produce rhythmic sounds.

elder - An older person.

fast - To go for a period without food.

feast - An elaborate meal often accompanied by a ceremony or entertainment.

gable - A triangular end of a building, especially the upper part of a building, or the sloping roof covering that part of a building.

headman - The chief of a band of Natives, especially in the Plateau Region.

immigrant - A person who comes to a country to live in it.

longhouse - A long, rectangular building that is large enough to hold several families or is used for community activities.

mammoth - Extinct hairy elephants living about 1,600,000 years ago.

medicine pouch - A small sack, usually of animal skin, which holds plants or objects that the pouch's owner believes to possess sacred meaning or magical powers.

Medicine Wheel - The concept that the "power of the world" moves in a circle.

migration - The movement of a person or group from one country or place to another.

missionary - A person who goes on a mission, such as an assignment to convert people to one's religious faith.

moccasin - A soft leather shoe without a heel.

Native American - A synonym for American Indian. Some Natives prefer it because it eliminates the mistaken term "Indian." Other Natives prefer the old term.

nomadic - Refers to people who move from place to place, usually in relation to the seasons and food supply, and have no fixed residence.

Plateau People - The Native Americans who inhabit the Columbia River Plateau. This plateau (tableland) extends from the Cascade Mountains in Washington and Oregon eastward, ending at the Rocky Mountains. It reaches northward into British Columbia and southward to California.

powwow - Originally referred to a shaman, a vision, or a gathering. Now, it means a cultural, social, and spiritual gathering to celebrate Native culture and pride.

reservation - A tract of public land set aside for a specific use. Tracts set aside for Natives. In Canada, they are called "reserves."

reserve - Canadian term for "reservation."

sage - A member of the mint family that is used in cooking and also as a medicinal herb.

shaman - Medicine man or woman.

sign language - A formal language that uses hand gestures instead of words.

sovereign nation - A community of people that has independent power and freedom.

spawn - To produce eggs, usually said of fish.

suumesh - A Salish word for spiritual power.

sweat lodge - A small building used for communal prayer and purification by sweating.

sweetgrass - One of four plants that Native Americans consider especially sacred (the others are sage, cedar, and tobacco).

tableland - A broad, relatively level, elevated area of land.

Thompson pit house - Partially buried, mounded houses of earth and brush, entered from the rooftop via a ladder.

tipi - A conical tent made of poles and skins.

tiwatitmas - Nez Perce word for spiritual power.

tobacco - A native American plant that belongs to the nightshade family.

treaty - An agreement or arrangement, usually written, made by negotiating.

tule - A type of large, tufted marsh plant, also called sedge or bulrush.

vision quest - The search a young Native undertakes, usually by going alone into the wilderness and spending one or more nights there. The individual fasts and prays for visions or dreams to reveal the spirits (usually animal spirits) that will provide lifetime guidance. The vision quest is an important part of the passage into adulthood.

Books of Interest

Barth, Kelly L. *Native Americans of the Northwest Plateau.* San Diego: Lucent Books, 2002.

Clark, Ella E., ed. *Indian Legends of the Pacific Northwest.* University of California Press, 1953.

Erdoes, Richard and Alfonso Ortiz, eds. *American Indian Myths and Legends.* New York: Pantheon, 1984

Faulk, Odie B. and Laura E Faulk. *The Modoc.* New York: Chelsea House, 1988.

Freedman, Russell. *Indian Chiefs.* New York: Holiday House, 1987.

Johnson, Michael. *Encyclopedia of Native Tribes of North America.* New York: Gramercy Books, 2001.

La Farge, Oliver. *The American Indian.* New York: Golden Press, 1956.

Nerburn, Kent, ed. *The Wisdom of the Native Americans.* Novato, Calif.: New World Library, 1999.

O'Dell, Scott and Elizabeth Hall. *Thunder Rolling in the Mountains.* Boston: Houghton Mifflin, 1992.

Sawyer, Don. *Where the Rivers Meet.* Winnipeg, Manitoba: Pemmican Publications Inc., 1988.

Schuster, Helen. *The Yakima.* New York, NY: Chelsea House, 1990.

Sherrow, Victoria. *Indians of the Plateau and Great Basin.* New York: Facts On File, 1992.

Thomasma, Kenneth and Jack Brouwer. *Pathki Nana: Kootenai Girl.* Jackson, Wyo.: Grandview Publishing, 1991.

Woodhead, Henry, series ed. *The American Indians.* Alexandria: Time Life Inc., 1992-94.

Yates, Diana. *Chief Joseph: Thunder Rolling Down from the Mountains.* New York: Ward Hill Press, 1992.

Children's Atlas of Native Americans. Chicago: Rand McNally & Co., 1996.

Good Web Sites to Begin Researching Native Americans

General Information Site with Links
http://www.nativeculture.com

Resources for Indigenous Cultures around the World
http://www.nativeweb.org/

Index of Native American Resources on the Internet
http://www.hanksville.org/NAresources/

News and Information from a Native American Perspective
http://www.indianz.com

An Online Newsletter Celebrating Native America
http://www.turtletrack.org

Native American History in the United States
http://web.uccs.edu/~history/index/nativeam.html

Internet School Library Media Center
http://falcon.jmu.edu/~ramseyil/native.htm

INDEX

Linda Thompson is a Montana native and a graduate of the University of Washington. She has been a teacher, writer, and editor in the San Francisco Bay Area for 30 years and now lives in Taos, New Mexico. She can be contacted through her web site, http://www.highmesaproductions.com